E-book edition published in 2020. ISBN: 978-1-7355074-3-9
Published by
Restorical LLC
5538 Sydonie Drive
Mount Dora, Florida 32757
Edited and formatted by Danielle Zimmerman and Clark Frogley

Summary:
Christmas Chicken is the amazing true story about a lost chicken that mysteriously showed up at Amy's house just before Christmas one year and how the family had an extra special experience that holiday season. Socks, the crazy house cat was never the same after that experience. Enjoy another beautiful and artistic story from Amy that will keep your children asking you to read it again and again.

Make sure and read other books by Amy as she shares her beautiful artistic talents to bring to life fun and educational stories enjoyed by young and old alike.

Restorical LLC is a company that is focused on the restoration of historic structures for use by the public. A portion of proceeds from all book sales are used to support Restorical's restoration efforts.

This book is dedicated to devoted fathers everywhere but especially to my father, Richard Webb Colyer, over whose left shoulder I spent countless hours watching artistic masterpieces come to life. His creativity made our childhood magical and formed the artist that made this book. Devoted not only to his own children, but to the children he spent 33 years teaching, he still found time to avidly read picture book after picture book to his little girls upon returning home. I shall never forget his captivating readings, or the love and time he was always so willing to deliver to all the children that have ever fallen into his path. God bless devoted fathers everywhere.

Once upon a Christmas, in upstate New York, a small homeless chicken set off on foot through the Schoharie Valley in the cold winter snow.

Her journey through the valley brought her to the old brick house a few days before Christmas. As she stopped to admire it from afar, a friendly cardinal swooped down and told her that the woman who used to live here liked to be called "Grandma Aa-ve" because she loved birds. The wee bird also mentioned that Grandma Aa-ve's great granddaughter, who was nicknamed "Fuzzy Duck" because of her downy-blonde, sticky-uppy hair, was in fact visiting here for Christmas. As the little bird was carrying on and on about ten chickens spending Christmas in the cellar one year, the homeless chicken decided she had heard enough. This was JUST the place for a bird to spend the holiday, so she approached the house.

The Chicken went to the front door and saw that there was no doorbell. To make matters worse, the doorknocker was holding up the Christmas wreath. She scratched her beak for a moment to think. At last she decided that she must fly up on the wreath to try to knock with the knocker, but when she did, nobody came to let her in.

The family was making a ruckus in the backroom. Fuzzy Duck was being tackled by big brother Adam while sister Danielle was singing for her audience and little cousin Isaa ate the TV.

No one could hear the chicken longing for the warmth of the home on that cold winter day.

Meanwhile, back on the wreath, the chicken continued to knock. The longer she sat there, the more she realized the wreath was actually pretty comfortable. It had all the makings of a good perch and the heat escaped through the windows of the house keeping her warm. She took off her travel clothes and announced, "this is quite nice!" The chicken felt regal on her Christmas roost and went to sleep.

The next day, while the chicken was still fast asleep, a special agent from the FBI paid the house a visit. Now this was not just any FBI agent, this was Fuzzy Duck's daddy! As he reached for the door handle, the frightened chicken flapped and squawked and nearly un-flapped the FBI!

Fuzzy Duck's daddy rushed inside and tried to explain to the family that there was a chicken perched on the Christmas wreath on the front door! Eagerly, everyone tiptoed to the front hall to see if his story was true or if he was trying to pull a Christmas trick.

To their delight, there was a chicken on the Christmas wreath! Instantly this festive chicken was named "Christmas Chicken" and she became the most popular houseguest that season.

Wanting to be good hosts, the grandchildren began to put feed down for Christmas Chicken to tempt her from her festive roost. While enjoying her meal one day, Christmas Chicken was discovered by the old house's cat.

Socks, or Crazy Cat, as the cat was also known, tried to torment Christmas Chicken. Most often, the chicken would just turn the other way. Sometimes, however, the chicken fought back by perching herself high above the wreath on the transom window that stretched across the top of the front door. The chicken knew she was safe up there, and this tortured Crazy Cat!

Crazy Cat spent day after day trying to launch herself from the marble table in the hall to the window above the door. Christmas Chicken, Fuzzy Duck, and the littlest grandchild, Isaac, found the cat's behavior amusing so they would watch...and watch...and watch....

At the end of the banister, she flew through the air, past Poppy's face, and onto the marble top table. From there, she hoped to launched herself up to the top of the window where the Chicken was perched. Unfortunately for the clueless cat, she instead splat against the window far below her target and landed unsuccessfully on the floor.

Not long after, Christmas came to the old brick house. The children lined up on the stairs waiting to be told it was okay to enter the backroom where a multitude of presents anxiously awaited them under the tree.

Littlest Isaac, being the first in line, was eager to say, "good morning" to Christmas Chicken before visiting the tree. He snuck away for a lengthy hello. The other children were excited to see what gifts were waiting for them, but all said, "Merry Christmas" to their feathered friend on their way to the back room.

Once united with the overstuffed tree, the family paused to focus on the blessings of giving and receiving. Poppy was joyful to receive his family in his old brick house that Christmas. Fuzzy Duck and Isaac were happy to receive toy after treasured toy.

Danielle was grateful to be able to give the gift of song, while brother Adam struggled to receive it. The family was a merry and festive sight all day, and well into the night.

Periodically, the family would check in with Christmas Chicken to make sure she was enjoying the holiday as much as they. Oh...how happy she looked on her merry wreath watching over her family that day.

One day, not long after Christmas, the time came for the children to leave the old brick house and return to their homes. Sadly, they said goodbye to their grandparents and to Christmas Chicken. No one wanted them to go, and the chicken hung her beak low.

Months passed and the chicken stayed on the outdated wreath. She was there for Valentine's Day...

President's Day...

And St. Patrick's Day in March...

Then, one spring day, just before Easter, things started looking familiar to the friendly Christmas Chicken. And so, she gathered her things, hopped off her perch, and disappeared just as quickly and mysteriously as she had come.

Perhaps the wee bird came back and told he
she would meet more roosters elsewhere in t
valley. After all, it was known that the loca
Parrott House fed and watered many old bire

Or, perhaps, she was so delighted with her Christmas family that she longed to start a family of her own. No one saw her come, and no one saw her go, but one thing was certain— her wreath was never the same again and neither was her Christmas family.

The End

Made in United States
Troutdale, OR
12/03/2023

15262641R00029